W9-BBM-529

DAISY GETS LOST

BY CHRIS RASCHKA

schwartz & wade books · new york

For Vladimir, Eugenia, and Tsetsa

Jacket art and interior illustrations copyright © 2013 by Chris Raschka
All rights reserved.
Published in the United States by Schwartz & Wade Books,
an imprint of Random House Children's Books,
a division of Random House, Inc., New York.
Schwartz & Wade Books and the colophon are
trademarks of Random House, Inc.
Visit us on the Web! randomhouse.com/kids
Educators and librarians, for a variety of teaching tools,
visit us at RHTeacherslibrarians.com
Library of Congress Cataloging-in-Publication Data
Raschka, Christopher.
Daisy gets lost / Chris Raschka.—First edition.
pages cm
Summary: A young dog experiences the fear of being lost
and the joys of being found when she becomes separated from her owner.
ISBN 978-0-449-81741-4 (trade) — ISBN 978-0-449-81742-1 (glb)
ISBN 978-0-449-81743-8 (ebook) [1. Dogs—Fiction. 2. Lost and found possessions—Fiction.
3. Stories without words.] I. Title. PZ7.R1814Dai 2013 [E]—dc23 2012049221
The illustrations in this book were rendered in ink, watercolor, and gouache.
MANUFACTURED IN CHINA
10 9 8 7 6 5 4 3 2 1
First Edition

Go get it, Daisy!

DAISY!